The children in Mrs May's class were painting. They had to do a portrait.

"I want you to paint someone's face," said Mrs May. "First, I will explain how to do it."

Mrs May drew an oval face. She drew
three lines across it and put one line down
the middle.

"The eyes are halfway down. The top of
the ears are level with the eyes," she said.

Chip was good at painting. He had
painted a portrait of Anneena.

"It's brilliant," said Nadim. "It looks just
like Anneena."

Mrs May put the finished portraits on the wall.

"Mine is rubbish," complained Wilf.

"No it's not," said Biff. "You just haven't got the ears quite right."

Chip had a sketch book. He had done a sketch of Mrs May.

"It's quite good," smiled Mrs May. "To get even better you need to practise. Try to draw as often as you can."

Wilf and Nadim went to play with Chip.
Chip's sketch book was in Biff's room. He
had done a sketch of Nadim.

"I'd like to be an artist when I grow up,"
said Chip.

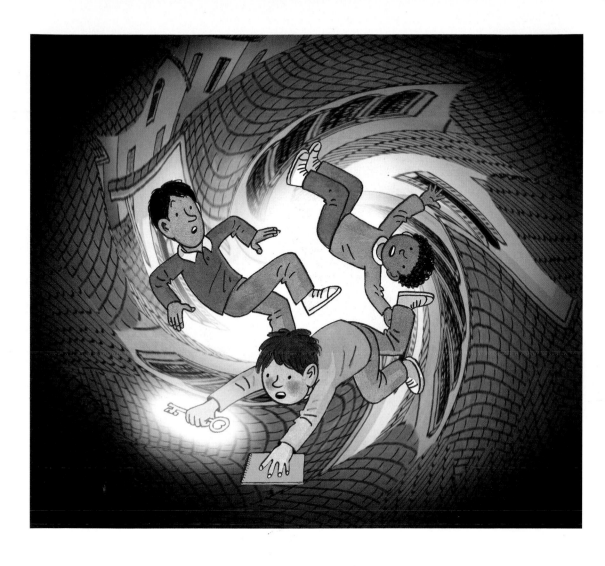

"I'll keep this," said Nadim. "In case you become a famous artist one day!"

Suddenly the magic key began to glow. The magic took the children on a new adventure.

The magic took the children back in time
to a city in Italy called Florence.

"I wonder why the key has brought us
here," said Chip.

Just then, they heard shouting. A man
was at an open window. He was shouting at
some men in the street.

"But, sir," called one of the men. "Your
picture is too big to go down the stairs."

"We could knock the staircase down,"
said another man. "But why not just cut six
inches off one end of the painting?"

"Impossible!" yelled the man. "I'm sure
these children have more sense than you."

He pointed at Wilf, Chip and Nadim.
"Children!" he shouted. "I am Sandro
Botticelli, the artist. Come up to my studio
and tell me which end to cut off my picture.
It has taken me two years to paint it."

"This picture is called 'Spring'," said Sandro. "Do you like it?"

Chip gasped. "It's a famous painting," he whispered. "I've seen it in a book."

Nadim was looking at the window.

"There's no need to take the staircase down," he said. "Knock out the window frame and lower the painting into the street."

"Ha!" said Sandro, clapping his hands. "Bravo! Children often know best."

"You want to be an artist, too?" Sandro
asked, looking at Chip's drawings. "You
need to work hard and draw all the time.
You must look, and study what you see."

"See! I am painting a portrait of a young man," Sandro went on. "I want you to help me. Put on this tunic so I can copy the folds in it."

Suddenly there was a loud thumping
noise and the house began to shake.

The jars and pots began to rattle. Some
fell on to the floor with a crash.

"Is it an earthquake?" gasped Chip.

"Ah!" groaned Sandro. "I cannot work like this. The man next door is a weaver. His looms make the walls shake."

"Go next door. Please beg him to stop
shaking my house," Sandro pleaded. "He
will not listen to me, but maybe he will listen
to you."

The weaver came to the door.

"Your looms are shaking the house of Sandro the artist," said Nadim. "He cannot paint his pictures."

The weaver showed them his looms.

"I weave fine cloth," he said "It is how I earn my living. And, in my own house, I can do what I please."

"Sandro, the artist, paints beautiful pictures. He paints fine portraits," said Chip. "That is his job."

"Bah! Weaving cloth is a *proper* job," the weaver replied.

"What did he say?" asked Sandro.

"In his own house he can do as he pleases," said Wilf.

"So!" said Sandro. "I need to teach him a lesson. Wait here."

Later, Sandro returned with some workmen. They had ropes and long thick poles of wood. On a cart was an enormous stone.

The men built a strong frame. Then
they pulled the boulder on to the edge of
Sandro's roof.

"Place it on the very edge," Sandro
ordered.

"It doesn't look very safe," said Wilf.
Sandro rubbed his hands.

"No. It is not safe," he said. "We will see what happens when the weaver's looms start working."

The weaver's looms began to shake Sandro's house. The enormous stone shook as well. It began to move.

"What are you doing?" cried the weaver. "The stone is unsafe. Remove it!"

"It will fall on to my house. It will crash through my roof," he wailed.

"Well," said Sandro. "In my own house, I can do what I please."

Nadim had an idea. He spoke to the
weaver. "Let the artist paint a portrait of
you wearing a cloak of your fine cloth. Rich
people will see it and want to buy from you."

"Why not work at different times?" Nadim added. "Then you will both be happy."

The two men shook hands. The weaver agreed to work in the mornings. The artist agreed to work in the afternoons.

"That was clever, Nadim," said Wilf.
Sandro began the portrait of the weaver
at once. He gave Chip one of his sketches.
Then the magic key began to glow.

"It was funny when the stone on the roof began to shake," laughed Wilf.

"I wonder if the portrait of the weaver will be in that book I saw at school," said Chip.

"This is a really good portrait," said Mrs May. "Did you draw it?"

"No, Sandro Botticelli did," said Chip.

"Very funny, Chip!" said Mrs May.